Merry Christmas 1997

With love to Carole

From Gail

THE ELDERS ARE WATCHING

# The Elders
# Are Watching

DAVID BOUCHARD

*Text*

ROY HENRY VICKERS

*Images*

RAINCOAST BOOKS

*Vancouver*

First edition published in 1990 by SummerWild Productions
Second edition published in 1994 by Raincoast Books

Third edition published in 1997 by

Raincoast Books
8680 Cambie Street
Vancouver, B.C.
V6P 6M9
(604) 323-7100

1 3 5 7 9 10 8 6 4 2

CANADIAN CATALOGUING IN PUBLICATION DATA

Bouchard, Dave, 1952-
The elders are watching

A poem.

ISBN 1-55192-110-3

1. Indians of North America – Poetry.  2. British Columbia in art.  I. Vickers, Roy Henry, 1946-  II. Title.

PS8553.O759E4 1997    C811'.54    C97-910576-5
PR9199.3.B617E4 1997

Printed and bound in Canada

# Thoughts

Revival, culture, heritage, environment, these are key words for this last decade of the century.

We continue to fight a battle to turn a tide of destruction that has been rising for many years and threatens to drown the family unit, our social structure, and our environment. We have been overly self-indulgent for too long, and it is time for change.

Change comes from understanding ourselves – our weaknesses, our strengths. That understanding can be fostered from knowledge of our past, our cultural heritage, and our environment. This priceless wisdom is available from our elders who, like us, received it from their ancestors.

We all have elders, ancestors, and a cultural heritage. Once we know our past, we have taken a step in understanding ourselves, and we will then be able to strengthen our truths, bringing about changes for the better.

Such changes can affect our many relationships – intimate ones, social and professional ones, and the one we have with our environment. These actions will help us to turn the tide, letting it wash over the land, healing those wrongs we have had a part in creating.


*Roy Henry Vickers*
*Tsartlip Reserve*
*Brentwood Bay, British Columbia*

# Whispers

The boy looked much the same as the other kids in his class. New faces arrived almost daily from far-away places, so it wasn't his appearance that made him different.

He had always tried his hardest, but try as he might, somehow he didn't seem to be able to get excited about the same things his classmates did. This year was no different.

And so, as in years gone by, his mother would please him greatly by taking him out of school for a time. Again she was sending him off to live with his grandfather, his Ya-A, to listen, to think, and to learn.

Ya-A would reintroduce him to the Wind, the Tree, and the Earth. Ya-A would speak of responsibilities and of rights. Ya-A would fascinate him with legends of the eagle, the whale, the raven, and the wolf.

Of all the tales his grandfather told, none captured his heart more than the stories of the Old Ones – the Elders. And as the stories slowly became part of him, by the seashore in the clear red sky of early evening, he began to see them.

They appeared as images suspended in the air, up toward the sun. Their lips were still, yet he heard them speak. Their message, like the words of his Ya-A, was clear and true, a message gone too long without being passed to other hearts.

He and his Ya-A would share the words of the Elders often with all those who cared to listen, with all those who cared at all.

*David Bouchard*
*North Vancouver, British Columbia*

They told me to tell you they believed you

When you said you would take a stand.

They thought that you knew the ways of nature.

They thought you respected the land.

1/50                    Look To The Mountain                    Roy H. Vickers
                                                                9/21/??

They want you to know that they trusted you

With the earth, the water, the air,

With the eagle, the hawk, and the raven,

The salmon, the whale, and the bear.

You promised you'd care for the cedar and fir,

The mountains, the sea, and the sky.

To the Elders these things are the essence of life.

Without them a people will die.

*They told me to tell you the time has come.*

*They want you to know how they feel.*

*So listen carefully, look toward the sun.*

*The Elders are watching.*

A MEETING OF CHIEFS

They wonder about risking the salted waters,

The ebb and flow of running tide.

You seem to be making mistakes almost daily.

They're angry, they're hurting, they cry.

1/50                              CHINOOK

The only foe the huge forest fears

Is man, not fire, nor pest.

There are but a few who've come to know

To appreciate nature's best.

They watch as you dig the ore from the ground.

You've gone much too deep in the earth.

The pits and scars are not part of the dream

For their home, for the place of their birth.

*They told me to tell you the time has come.*

*They want you to know how they feel.*

*So listen carefully, look toward the sun.*

*The Elders are watching.*

They say you hunt for the thrill of the kill.

First the buffalo, now the bear.

And that you know just how few there are left,

And yet you don't seem to care.

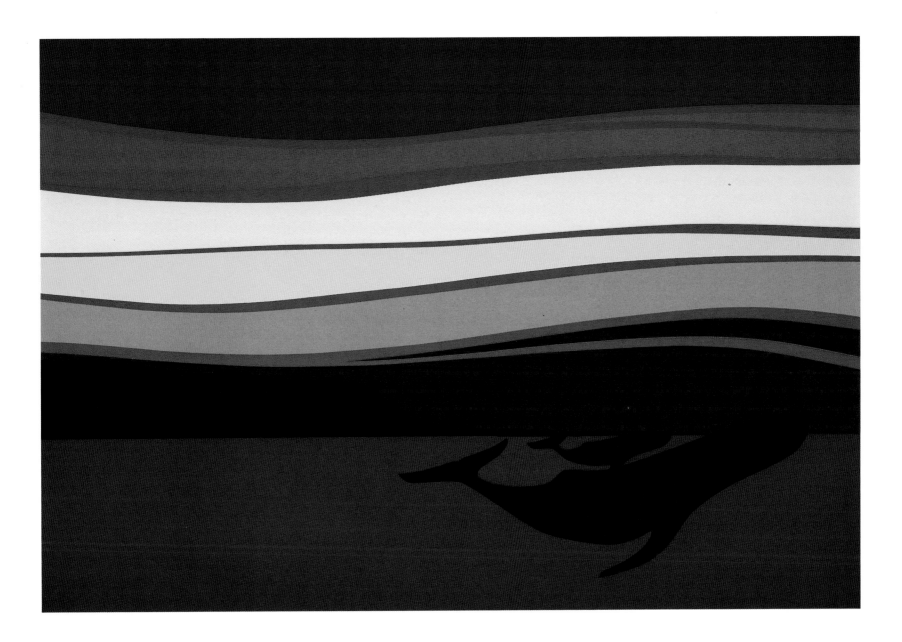

They have no problem with fishing for sport.

There are lots of fish in the sea.

It is for the few who will waste a catch,

For you, they are speaking through me.

You said you needed the tree for its pulp,

You'd take but a few, you're aware

Of the home of the deer, the wolf, the fox,

Yet so much of their land now stands bare.

*They told me to tell you the time has come.*

*They want you to know how they feel.*

*So listen carefully, look toward the sun.*

*The Elders are watching.*

They're starting to question the things that you said

About bringing so much to their land.

You promised you'd care for their daughters and sons,

That you'd walk with them hand in hand.

A/P III/8          Dreams of the Past          Roy H. Vickers
                                               MAR/84

But with every new moon you seem to be

More concerned with your wealth than the few

Women and children, their bloodline, their heartbeat,

Who are now so dependent on you.

VISIONS OF THE FUTURE

You are offering to give back bits and pieces

Of the land they know to be theirs.

Don't think they're not grateful, it's just hard to say so

When wondering just how much you care.

1/50          NINSTINTS

*They told me to tell you the time has come.*

*They want you to know how they feel.*

*So listen carefully, look toward the sun.*

*The Elders are watching.*

1/50                                    CARMANAH                                    Roy H. Vick
                                                                                    9/12/09

Now, friend, be clear and understand

Not everything's dark and glum.

They are seeing things that are making them smile,

And that's part of the reason I've come.

Going To The Potlatch

The colour green has come back to the land.

It's for people who feel like me.

For people who treasure what nature gives,

For those who help others to see.

And there are those whose actions show.

They see the way things could be.

They do what they can, give all that they have

Just to save one ancient tree.

*They told me to tell you the time has come.*

*They want you to know how they feel.*

*So listen carefully, look toward the sun.*

*The Elders are watching.*

Of all the things that you've done well,

The things they are growing to love,

It's the sight of your home, the town that you've built.

They can see it from far up above.

Like the sun when it shines, like the full moon at night,

Like a hundred totems tall,

It has brightened their sky and that's partially why

They've sent me to you with their call.

Now I've said all the things that I told them I would.

I hope I am doing my share.

If the beauty around us is to live through this day,

We'd better start watching – and care.

*They told me to tell you the time is now.*

*They want you to know how they feel.*

*So listen carefully, look toward the sun.*

*The Elders are watching.*